LET'S WORK IT OUT™

How to deal with BULLIES

Jonathan Kravetz

PowerKiDS press
New York

Published in 2007 by The Rosen Publishing Group, Inc.
29 East 21st Street, New York, NY 10010

First Edition

Editor: Jennifer Way
Book Design: Ginny Chu
Layout Design: Kate Laczynski
Photo Researcher: Sam Cha

Photo Credits: Cover, p.1 © Getty Images; pp. 4, 6, 18 © Corbis; p. 10 image copyright Elena Elisseeva, 2006, used under license from Shutterstock, Inc.; pp. 8, 12, 14, 16, 20 © istockphoto.

Library of Congress Cataloging-in-Publication Data

Kravetz, Jonathan.
   How to deal with Bullies / Jonathan Kravetz. — 1st ed.
      p. cm. — (Let's work it out)
   Includes index.
   ISBN-13: 978-1-4042-3670-7 (library binding)
   ISBN-10: 1-4042-3670-8 (library binding)
   1. Bullying–Juvenile literature. I. Title.
   BF637.B85K73 2007
   302.3'4—dc22
                                        2006025640

Manufactured in the United States of America

Contents

Bullies beat up others because they want to feel like they have power over them. This book will show you ways to deal with bullying.

Bullies

A bully is a person who hurts other people. The bully does this either **physically** or with words. Bullies hurt others to try to prove that they have power.

In school bullies might **threaten** to hurt their **targets** in order to take something they want. A bully might also wait for a target after school to beat him or her up. In this book we will learn about the different types of bullies and how to deal with them.

Sometimes more than one bully will pick on the same person.

When Is It Bullying?

Everyone jokes and plays around with each other from time to time. This is fine as long as everyone feels safe and no one gets hurt. However, when one person uses unwanted physical **contact** or hurts another person's feelings, it becomes bullying.

Bullies are often stronger and bigger than their targets. They use their size to scare or hurt others. Bullying can happen between friends, but it often happens between children who are not friends.

Kids who are targets of bullies can feel very alone. This can lead to feelings of low self-esteem.

Feeling Bad

You might not guess this, but many bullies feel bad about themselves. They suffer from **low self-esteem** because they feel like no one cares for or likes them. They might have trouble at home with their family. Bullying others gives the bully a sense of power. They are making someone feel as bad as they feel.

Sadly the targets of bullies also end up suffering from low self-esteem. They also feel unliked or powerless. Children with low self-esteem, whether they are the bullies or the bullied, can feel bad long after the bullying has ended.

Relationship bullies try to keep others from being friends with their target.

Types of Bullies

There are three main types of bullies. These are physical bullies, **verbal** bullies, and **relationship** bullies. Physical bullies hit and kick to hurt their targets. These bullies often get more physical as they get older.

Verbal bullies use words to **humiliate** other children. Sometimes verbal bullying hurts more than physical bullying because the bullied person can remember hurtful words for a long time.

Relationship bullies try to get their peers to leave out a certain person from their group. This happens when children, often girls, spread **rumors** about others to keep an ex-friend out of a group.

Bullies often have low self-esteem. Their bad feelings about themselves come out as anger toward others.

Why Do People Bully?

Bullies want power. Because they suffer from low self-esteem, they believe that by bullying others they can make themselves feel stronger or better than the person they bully. Making someone else feel as bad as they do is the only way they know to feel good about themselves.

They may also be trying to cover up how bad they feel about themselves. Sometimes bullies are mean because someone in their life is mean to them. A bully might be treated badly by a sibling, by older kids at school, or even by a parent.

Kids who have been bullied sometimes carry their fear of being bullied for a long time.

The Bully's Target

Bullies often pick on kids who are different from the other kids. Bullies might pick on the new kid or on kids who have fewer friends. They might pick on kids who look and act different from other kids. Children who become targets often seem **defenseless** to the bully. This makes the bully think he or she can get away with picking on them.

Many targets of bullies are scared to report how they are being treated. They might be afraid of making the bullying worse or of looking like a tattletale. No one who is bullied is "asking for it."

16

Talking to parents or other trusted adults can help you deal with bullying. You can talk about your feelings and they can help you feel safe.

What If You Are Being Bullied?

The best way to handle a bully is to try not to **react**. Some bullies leave people alone when they do not get the reaction they want from their target.

If that does not work, you should walk away with your head held high. This shows the bully that you have not let his or her actions hurt you. Even if that is not totally true, doing it might be the first step to helping you feel better. Whatever you do, you should tell a trusted adult about the bully to keep further bullying from happening to you or to someone else.

Sticking by your friends is called the buddy system. If you stand together, you can help each other.

What If a Friend Is Being Bullied?

Sometimes bullying takes place in front of other kids. These kids might feel scared of the bully or glad that they are not the target and do nothing. What should you do if your friend or your classmates are being bullied?

You and your friends and classmates can stick together. This is called the buddy system. With the buddy system, each person will feel less alone. A bully is less likely to pick on a group of people who stand together and tell him or her to stop. Being part of a group can also help build self-esteem.

20

If you are bullying others, you should ask yourself why you feel so angry. You can ask a trusted adult for help in better dealing with these feelings.

What If You Are a Bully?

If you think you might be a bully, you should take time to think about why. Are you unhappy? Do you get along with others? Are you being bullied by other people? How can you learn how to feel better about yourself without bullying others?

It might sound hard, but try talking to an adult whom you trust. He or she might help you with your problems and show you other ways to feel better about yourself. Try becoming part of groups, such as sports teams or clubs, in which you get to meet new friends. These are positive ways to build your self-esteem.

Changing a Bully's Behavior

Bullies need to learn why they bully and they need help from their families. Parents are often the reason children become bullies. Parents need to learn why certain **behaviors** of theirs or of their children are not healthy.

Many schools now have antibullying **programs** to help change bullies' behavior and to help kids who are being bullied. If there is not an antibullying program at your school, you might ask a trusted teacher about starting one.

Glossary

behaviors (bee-HAY-vyurz) Ways to act.

contact (KON-takt) The touching or meeting of people or things.

defenseless (dih-FENS-les) Cannot save itself from being hurt.

humiliate (HYOO-mih-lee-ayt) To make someone else feel very bad about himself or herself.

low self-esteem (LOW self-uh-STEEM) Little happiness with oneself.

physically (FIH-zih-kul-ee) Having to do with the body.

programs (PROH-gramz) Meetings that are held by a group for a purpose.

react (re-AKT) To feel or act after something happens.

relationship (rih-LAY-shun-ship) A connection, usually with friends and family.

rumors (ROO-murz) Stories that are heard by people without knowing if they are true.

targets (TAR-gits) People who are the object of a bully's attention.

threaten (THREH-tun) To possibly cause hurt.

verbal (VER-bul) Using words.

Index

C
contact, 7

F
family, 9
feelings, 7
friend(s), 7, 15, 19

L
low self-esteem, 9, 13

P
parent(s), 13, 22
peers, 11
physical bullies, 11

R
relationship bullies, 11
rumors, 11

S
school, 5, 13, 22

sibling, 13
size, 7

T
target(s), 5, 7, 11, 15, 17, 19
tattletale, 15
trouble, 9

V
verbal bullies, 11

Web Sites

Due to the changing nature of Internet links, PowerKids Press has developed an online list of Web sites related to the subject of this book. This site is updated regularly. Please use this link to access the list:
www.powerkidslinks.com/lwio/bullie/